SHARON CREECH · DAVID DIAZ

Who's That Baby?

NEW-BABY SONGS

JOANNA COTLER · BOOKS
An Imprint of HarperCollinsPublishers

Who's That Baby?

Text copyright © 2005 by Sharon Creech

Illustrations copyright © 2005 by David Diaz

Manufactured in China. All rights reserved.

No part of this book may be used or reproduced in any manner

whatsoever without written permission except in the case of brief

quotations embodied in critical articles and reviews.

For information address HarperCollins Children's Books,

a division of HarperCollins Publishers, 1350 Avenue of the

Americas, New York, NY 10019.

www.harperchildrens.com

Library of Congress Cataloging-in-Publication Data

Creech, Sharon.

Who's that baby? : new-baby songs / Sharon Creech ;

David Diaz.— 1st ed.

p.   cm.

Summary: Short poems and songs reflect the life of a

newborn baby, as he or she meets various relatives and

learns about the world.

ISBN 0-06-052939-3 — ISBN 0-06-052940-7 (lib. bdg.)

1. Infants—Juvenile poetry. 2. Children's poetry,

American. [1. Babies—Poetry. 2. American poetry.]

I. Diaz, David, ill. II. Title.

PS3553.R3373B33 2005   2003012613

811'.54—dc22

Typography by David Diaz

1 2 3 4 5 6 7 8 9 10

❖

First Edition

Who's That Baby?

Who are you, baby
newly born
who's this little babe?

What are you thinking
inside that head
and what do you dream
when you go to bed?

And what will you look like
and will you have hair
and will you be tall
or dark or fair?

And what will you wonder
and what will cause tears
and what will you feel
and think and fear?

Who are you, baby
newly born
who's this little babe?

Baby in the Basket

A tisket, a tasket
a baby in the basket!

I'm so snug
and I'm so warm
I'm so cute
I'm just born!

A tisket, a tasket
a baby in the basket!

Pearly Girl

Oh, I am a little girl
as treasured as a pearl
and a bella, bella pearl am I.

With my soft, soft skin
and my bright, bright eyes
and my wiggles and my waves
and my sweet, sweet smile
a bella, bella pearl am I.

Oh, they sing me songs
all day and night
and they hold me tight
all day and night
because they love this pearl
this pearly girl
a bella, bella pearl am I.

Joy Boy

Oh, I am a little boy
so full of joy,
a bello, bello boy am I.

With my soft, soft skin
and my bright, bright eyes
and my wiggles and my waves
and my sweet, sweet smile
a bello, bello boy am I.

Oh, they sing me songs
all day and night
and they hold me tight
all day and night
because they love this boy
this boy of joy
a bello, bello boy am I.

Baby Burrito

I'm a little burrito
look at me

a baby burrito
in a little quilt-o
in my mama's arms . . .

and Daddy's here, too
all wrapped up
a daddy burrito
with big feet-o . . .

and there's our doggie
sandwiched in between
a doggie burrito
looks so neat-o . . .

That's our family:
a burrito bunch
a burrito-rito bunch!

Football Baby

My daddy thinks
I am a football.

I think that
he is mistaken.

I hope that
someone will tell him

that I am a baby
his little sweet baby.

. . . I am not
a little pigskin.

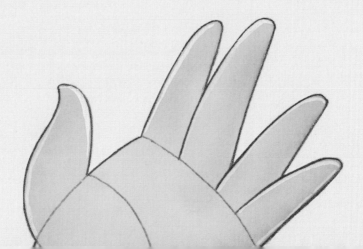

Two Big Grandmas

Two big grandmas
looking at me
smiling their great big smiles

They say
"Ooh!" and "Ahh!"
and "Aww!" and "Oh!"

(Not very big vocabularies
for two big grandmas . . .)

And I am waving
at my two smiling grandmas
with the not-very-big vocabularies

Waving, waving, waving
and I am thinking:
"Hi there, grandmas!
You love me
don'tcha?"

And they say
"Ooh!" and "Ahh!"
and "Aww!" and "Oh!"

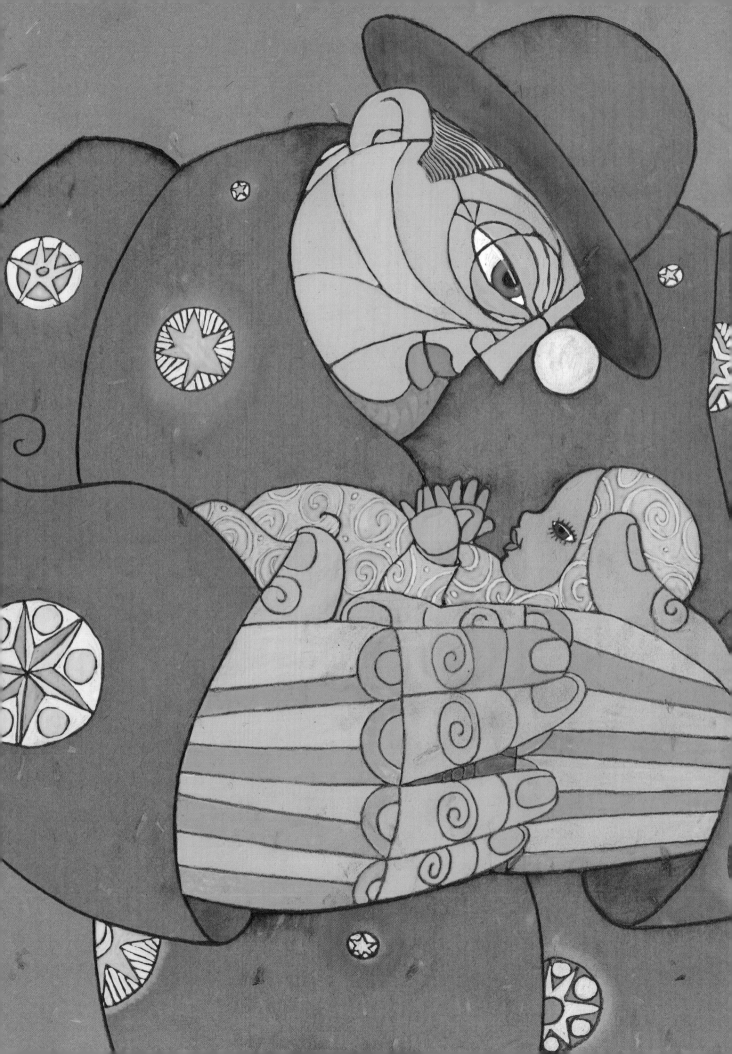

Grandpa

My grandpa is very large
I am quite small in his arms

My grandpa is very soft
His voice is low and deep

He holds me so so gently
And whispers little things:

Hi, little one.
I'm your grandpa.
Don't be afraid.
I am here.

Leaky Baby

Leaky baby
leaky baby
I'm a leaky baby.

Blurping milk
on Mommy's clothes
and Daddy's clothes

on their shoulders
on their laps
in their hair

on the couches
and the rugs
and the beds
and the chairs.

Diapers leaking
everywhere

Saliva dripping
down my chin.

Leaky baby
leaky baby
what a leaky baby!

Books

They plop me on their laps
and open up the books
and read-read-read
in up-and-down voices.

I have no idea
what they are saying
but I like the sounds
of the up-and-down voices.

And I love the swirly pictures
which I try to touch
and lick

but they tell me
I should not
eat
the book.

Banana Baby

They say it's cold outside
brr brr brr
and so they wrap me
in a warm sleeper
and squeeze a hat
on my perfect bald head
and they ease me into
my fuzzy yellow bunting
and I look like
a stuffed banana.

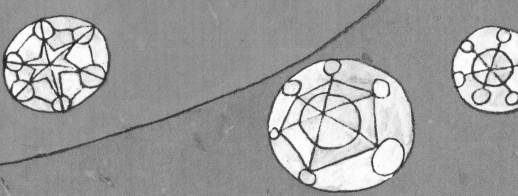

Photos

I am sitting
on my mommy's lap
gazing at pictures
of me me me!

Me awake
me asleep
me in diapers
me in fleece
me in tub
me in crib

Me with Mommy
me with Daddy
me with Grandma
me with Grandpa

Me with duck
me with dolly
me with bear
me with doggie

Me in yellow
me in white
me in spots
me in stripes

Me upon my mommy's lap
wondering what they did
before there was
me me me!

Why Do You Love Me?

I wonder why you love me.

I sometimes cry an awful lot
I sometimes puke on you
I often need my diaper changed
I keep you up at night

And still
you kiss me, hug me, kiss me
and while I sleep
you gaze at me
(you think I do not know)

And put your hands
upon my chest
lightly, lightly
to feel my breathing
and my heart beating.

It is a good thing
that you can love me
even though I do
the things I do.

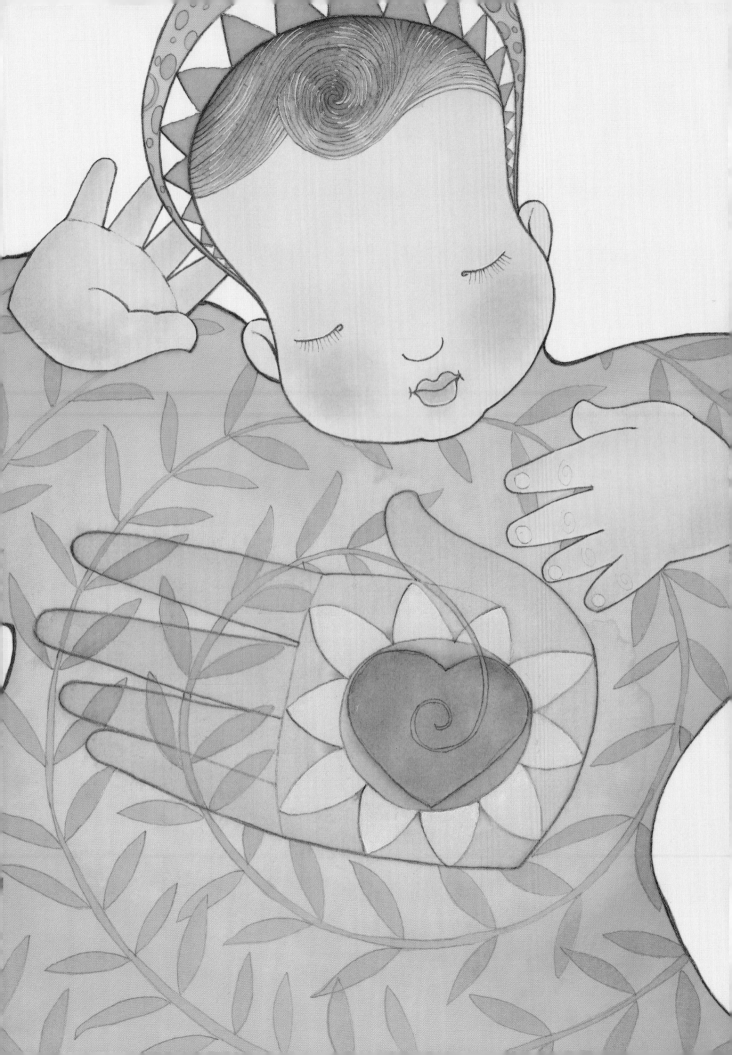